Remembering

The Story of a Soldier

Virginia Mayo

HUTCHINSON

London Sydney Auckland Johannesburg

Dedicated to the memory of my uncle, Private Albert W. Salter
1920 - 1944

First published in 1996
1 3 5 7 9 10 8 6 4 2
© Virginia Mayo 1996

Virginia Mayo has asserted her right under
the Copyright, Designs and Patents Act, 1988,
to be identified as the author of this work

First published in the United Kingdom in 1996 by
Hutchinson Children's Books
Random House UK Limited
20 Vauxhall Bridge Road, London SW1V 2SA

Random House Australia (Pty) Limited
20 Alfred Street, Milsons Point, Sydney
New South Wales 2061, Australia

Random House New Zealand Limited
18 Poland Road, Glenfield
Auckland 10, New Zealand

Random House South Africa (Pty) Limited
PO Box 337, Bergvlei, South Africa

Random House UK Limited Reg. No. 954009

A CIP catalogue record for this book
is available from the British Library

ISBN: 0 09 176687 7

Printed in Hong Kong

One day we went for a walk with Grandad.

We found a lovely garden...

... and then a statue of a soldier. Grandad said it was for the men who had died in the war. All around were garlands of poppies.

Lizzie and I bought a poppy each. Then we walked back to Grandad's house for tea.

There was a picture of a soldier on the wall. Nanny said he was our Great Uncle Albert, who was killed in the war.

We went to bed, but we didn't go to sleep. We thought we heard a noise and crept downstairs. Someone was in the living room. Carefully, we opened the door.

The room looked different. A man was sitting at the table.
He looked like someone we knew.

Lizzie said, 'Do you live here?'

'No,' he said softly.
'I lived a long time ago.'

'Can you stay
with us?'

'No ... I can't ...
I have to go.'

He opened a door and we followed him through.

We were in a meadow.

There were some more soldiers. Some were playing cards, others were just waiting.

Something seemed to be worrying them.
Their officer was calling.

Our soldier said to us,
'Goodbye Lizzie and
Robert. You must go
back now.'

The soldiers disappeared into
the fog.

The sounds of firing and battle stopped. For a long time we watched the empty town, waiting for the soldiers to return.

But they never came back.

Then we turned around. The field was full of poppies. I sat down and Lizzie picked a flower.

Suddenly we were back at Grandad's...

... and we gave the poppy to the soldier in the frame.